CHIKE
and the River

Chinua Achebe

CHIKE
and the River

ILLUSTRATIONS BY EDEL RODRIGUEZ

ANCHOR BOOKS
A Division of Random House, Inc.
New York

AN ANCHOR BOOKS ORIGINAL, AUGUST 2011

Library of Congress Cataloging-in-Publication Data
Achebe, Chinua.
Chike and the river / by Chinua Achebe ; [illustrations by Edel Rodriguez].
p.   cm.
ISBN: 978-0-307-47386-8
1. City and town life—Nigeria—Fiction.
2. Niger River—Fiction.   3. Blacks—Nigeria—Fiction.
4. Nigeria—Fiction.   5. Adventure and adventurers—Fiction.   I. Rodriguez, Edel, ill.   II. Title.
PZ7.A174Ch 2011
[Fic]—dc22   2010050595

Book design by Debbie Glasserman

www.anchorbooks.com

Printed in the United States of America
10   9   8   7   6   5   4   3   2   1

For my daughter, Chinelo,
and for all my nephews and nieces

CHIKE
and the River

1
Chike Leaves His Village

Chike lived with his mother and two sisters in the village of Umuofia. His father had died many years ago. His mother worked very hard to feed and clothe her three children and to send them to school. She grew most of the food they ate—yams, cassava, maize, beans, plantains, and many green vegetables. She also traded in dry fish, palm oil, kerosene, and matches.

Chike was now eleven years old, and he had never left his village. Then one day his mother told him that he would be going to Onitsha in the new year to live with his uncle who was a clerk in one of the firms there. At first Chike was full of joy. He was tired of living in a bush village and wanted to see a big city. He had heard many wonderful stories about Onitsha. His uncle's servant, Michael, had told him that there was a water tap in the very compound where they lived. Chike said this was impossible but Michael had sworn to its truth by wetting his first finger on his tongue and pointing it to the sky. Chike was too thrilled for words. So he would no longer wake up early in the morning to go to the stream. The trouble with their village stream was that the way to it was very rough and stony, and sometimes children fell and broke their water-pots. In Onitsha Chike would be free from all those worries. Also he would live in a house with an iron roof instead of his mother's poor hut of mud and thatch. It all sounded so wonderful.

But when the time actually came for Chike to leave his mother and sisters he began to cry. His sisters cried too, and even his mother had signs of tears in her eyes. She placed one hand on his head and said, "Go well, my son. Listen to whatever your uncle says and obey him. Onitsha is a big city, full of dangerous people and kidnappers. Therefore do not wander about the

city. In particular do not go near the River Niger;
many people get drowned there every year . . ."

She gave Chike many other words of advice. He
nodded his head and sniffed because his nose was
running. Chike's nose always ran when he cried.

"Stop crying," said his mother. "Remember, you
are now a big boy, and big boys don't cry."

Chike wiped his eyes with the back of his hand.
Then he took up his small wooden box which his
mother had bought from James Okeke, the local
carpenter. Inside it were his few clothes and school-
books.

"Let us go," said his uncle who had been waiting
patiently. "If we don't hurry now, we shall miss the
lorry."*

Chike set the box on his head and followed his
uncle. They were going to the main road half a mile
away to take the lorry that passed by their village
to Onitsha. It was a very old lorry called Slow-
and-Steady. It always had great difficulty going up
any hill. Whenever it got to a steep hill the driver's
mate would jump down and walk behind it with the
big wooden wedge. Sometimes the passengers were

---

* A *lorry* is a truck.

asked to climb down and help push the lorry. The forty-mile journey to Onitsha took Slow-and-Steady more than three hours. Sometimes it broke down completely; then the journey might take a whole day or more.

Chike was, however, lucky on the day he made the journey. Slow-and-Steady was in good form and did not break down at all. It only stopped after every hill to take a tin of water.

2

Chike in Onitsha

At first Onitsha looked very strange to Chike. He could not say who was a thief or kidnapper and who was not. In Umuofia every thief was known, but here even people who lived under the same roof were strangers to one another. Chike was told by his uncle's servant that sometimes a man died in one room and his neighbor in the next room would be playing his gramophone. It was all very strange.

But as the months passed Chike began to feel at home in Onitsha. He made friends at school and became very popular among them. His best friend was called Samuel. They were about the same age.

Samuel was very good at football.* He could dribble past any opponent. Whenever he played particularly well his admirers clapped and shouted, "S.M.O.G.! S.M.O.G.!"

S.M.O.G. was Samuel's nickname which he gave himself. His full name was Samuel Maduka Obi; so his initials were S.M.O. Then one day he saw that if he added a "G" to his initials he would become S.M.O.G. He immediately did so. In Onitsha the letters S.M.O.G. were said to bring good luck because they stood for Save Me O God.

Chike was also pretty good at football and very soon his friends gave him a nickname too. They called him "Chiks The Boy." Chike liked the name very much and wrote it in his new reader.

It was from Samuel that Chike first heard how easy it was to cross the River Niger and come back again.

"I have done it many times on the ferryboat," Samuel told him. "All you need is sixpence to go over and sixpence to return. Finish."

"But I have no sixpence," said Chike.

"What?" said Samuel, "a big boy like you has no sixpence. Don't let people hear it. It is too shameful."

* Soccer.

Chike was really ashamed and so he told a lie to cover his shame. He said, "It's not that I don't have money. I have plenty but my uncle keeps it for me."

"Then tell your uncle to give you one shilling out of it," said Samuel. "What is the use of having money that you cannot spend?"

"I shall ask him sometime," replied Chike, "but not yet."

"Time and tide wait for no man," said Samuel in English. It was their teacher's favorite saying. "And have you not heard," continued Samuel, "that they are building a bridge across the river? They will finish it soon and then there will be no more ferries."

Chike had indeed heard of the bridge they were building. He was greatly troubled by what Samuel said.

A few days later Chike's friends were again talking about the river. They spoke about Asaba on the other side.

"Do you know," said Samuel to Chike, "that as soon as you step out of the ferry in Asaba you are in Midwestern Nigeria?"

The others agreed excitedly. They all had been to the Midwest. "And do you know," said another boy whose name was Ezekiel, "that once you are in Asaba it is *one way* to Lagos?"

"Yes," said Samuel. "Lagos. Second-to-London. I have not been to Lagos. But I know Asaba which is poor-man's Lagos."

His companions laughed. Samuel sometimes talked like a grown man; this was one of the reasons why he was so popular with his companions.

Chike's mind was far away—in Midwestern Nigeria. He liked such flowing phrases. Midwestern Nigeria, A Midsummer Night's Dream, The Isle of Man.

3
Chike on the Banks of the River

Chike's uncle was a very strict man. He rarely spoke and never laughed except when he drank cold beer or palm wine with his neighbor, Mr. Nwaba, or with one of his few friends. He did not like to see Chike playing with other children. He called it a waste of time. In his opinion children should spend their time reading and doing sums. His neighbor, Mr. Nwaba, agreed with him. His children played only when he was not around.

Chike had a different opinion. According to his teacher: *All work and no play makes Jack a dull boy*. Chike agreed completely with this saying. He wanted to tell his uncle about it but lacked the courage.

One Saturday morning Chike felt very brave. He stood behind his uncle and asked for a shilling. His uncle, who was shaving, turned round. He had a small mirror in his left hand and razor in his right. His lower face was all covered in white soapsuds.

"What do you want a shilling for?" he asked.

"I want to go on the ferry to Asaba before they build the bridge," replied Chike, fearlessly.

"Have you gone off your mind?" asked his uncle in great annoyance. "Run away from here before I count to three. One! Two! . . ."

Chike fled from him. For the first time in many months tears filled his eyes.

"I will write a letter to my mother to send me the money," he said to himself. But then he remembered that his mother had warned him not to go near the river. So he became very sad.

Later that day his uncle told Mr. Nwaba about Chike's request. Mr. Nwaba put down his glass of palm wine and laughed. Then he said: "Asaba is too near. Why does he not want to go to Lagos?"

Chike's uncle was as yet unmarried. His servant, Michael, was a very big boy and he did all the difficult work in the house. He split firewood, went to the market, cooked, washed clothes and ironed them.

Chike washed the plates after meals and sometimes swept the rooms.

They lived in two rooms. His uncle slept in one of them and kept all his boxes there. The soup-pot and other cooking vessels were hidden away under his huge iron bed. The other room had chairs, a round table in the center, framed photographs on the walls, a radio on the wooden pedestal in one of the four corners, a bookcase against the wall, and many other things. It was here that Michael and Chike slept. At night they moved the round table aside and spread their mat on the floor.

Chike did not like sleeping on the floor and he longed for the bamboo bed in his mother's hut. There were other things he did not like. For example there were bedbugs on their mat. Sometimes Michael sprinkled kerosene on the mat to kill them off. But after a few days they were there again. Another thing Chike did not like was the large crowd of other tenants living in the same house. There were ten rooms in the house and more than fifty men, women, and children living in them. Many families lived in one room. Because there were so many strangers living together they were always quarreling about firewood and about sweeping the yard or scrubbing the bathroom and the latrines.

There were only two latrines in the yard for the fifty people. One was for adults and the other for children. Both were filthy but the children's was worse. It swarmed with flies bigger than any Chike had ever seen at Umuofia. They revolted him. And so he learnt that a big town was not always better than a village. But there were things he liked in Onitsha.

Every Saturday Michael went to the big market to buy provisions. Sometimes when he had many things to buy he took Chike with him. Chike did not help in the buying but in carrying some of the things home. He did not mind this at all. In fact he liked it. While Michael bargained with the traders Chike stood aside watching the great river as it flowed peacefully down to the sea. He watched the fishermen in their canoes coming down the river or struggling up against it. Some of the canoes were houseboats; they had roofs of thatch over them. Chike was told that the fishermen lived for weeks or months in these boats.

But what Chike liked most was to watch the big ferryboats. They looked enormous to him. He wondered what big ships would look like. His class teacher had told them that big ships could only be seen at Lagos, Port Harcourt, or Burutu. But surely these ferryboats at Onitsha were big enough. What did anyone want bigger boats for? Even the canoes were big enough for some people to live in.

The more Chike saw the ferryboats the more he wanted to make the trip to Asaba. But where would he get the money? He did not know. Still, he hoped.

"One day is one day," he said, meaning that one day he would make the journey, come what may.

4

Ezekiel, the Spoilt Child

Chike was so anxious to find the money for his trip across the river that he very nearly went into bad ways.

One of his friends called Ezekiel was a very bad boy. Like Chike, Ezekiel was his mother's only son. He had four sisters. Ezekiel's mother was a well-to-do trader who sold cloth in the Onitsha market and made much profit. But she was not a wise mother. She allowed Ezekiel to do whatever he liked. So he became a spoilt child. His mother had three servants who did all the housework. Sometimes Ezekiel's sisters were asked to wash plates or draw water from the public tap. But he never did any work. His mother said that housework was only for servants and for girls. So Ezekiel was developing into a lawless little imp. He would sneak quietly to the soup-pot at night and search with his fingers for pieces of fish and meat. By morning the soup would go sour and Ezekiel's mother would punish the servants. One day one of his sisters caught him red-handed. His fingers were covered with egusi soup. But Ezekiel denied it all, and his mother believed him.

When Ezekiel grew bigger he began to steal little sums of money from his mother. With this he bought akara, mai-mai, and groundnuts at break. Sometimes he was even able to buy whole packets of sweet biscuits or a tin of corned beef and a shilling loaf of bread.

Needless to say he was very popular at school. He was called Tough Boy and his friends thought the world of him. Of course they had no idea that he stole from his mother.

Then one day Ezekiel did something really awful. When he told his friends about it they thought it was very clever until their headmaster told them how wrong it was.

Ezekiel had somehow got hold of the names of three boys in England who wanted Nigerian pen-friends. He wrote to them asking one to send him money, another to send him a camera, and the third to send him a pair of shoes. He drew a pattern of his right foot on a piece of paper and sent it along. He promised each of the boys a leopard skin in return. Of course he had no intention of fulfilling the promise. For one thing he had never seen a leopard skin in his life.

After a month he received a ten-shilling postal order from one of the boys. He showed it to his mother and she called him Clever Boy, which was one of the many fond names she had given him. Then she took him to the post office to cash the postal order.

Ezekiel told his friends at school about his exploits and they were all highly impressed. "Tough Boy! Tough Boy!" was shouted on all sides.

The same day many other boys rushed off letters to England. Chike obtained two addresses but could not write straightaway because he had no money to buy postage stamps. He decided that as soon as he could find sixpence he would write to England and ask for ten shillings or even one pound. Then he would cross and recross the Niger as often as he liked. He thought how rich England

19

must be when even a little boy could part with ten shillings. He had seen the letter the boy wrote to Ezekiel. His name was John Smith and he was aged twelve. Imagine that! Only twelve and yet he had ten shillings to throw away. What did he want a leopard skin for? English people must be crazy, thought Chike.

It was fortunate for Chike that he had no money to buy a postage stamp. If he had he would have been in serious trouble along with Ezekiel and the others.

One day at school the headmaster called Ezekiel out and took him to his office. Later he sent for five other boys. They were away for about an hour. Then the school bell rang and classes stopped. The headmaster, stern and full of anger, spoke to the school.

"I have just received a letter from the headmaster of a school in England," he said and held up a blue letter for all to see. "The content of this letter has filled me with shame," he continued. "I did not know that among us here are thieves and robbers, wolves in sheep's clothing . . ." He spoke at length about Ezekiel's crime. "Think of the bad name which you have given this school," he said, turning to Ezekiel and the five boys; they were all looking at the floor. "Think of the bad name you have given Nigeria, your motherland," he said, and the whole school sighed. "Think how the school in England will always remember Nigeria as a country of liars and thieves because of these six scallywags here." Some of the pupils laughed because of the new word *scallywag*.

"Yes, they are scallywags," said the headmaster, "and they have spoilt your name in England. Some of you will go to study in England when you grow up. What do you think will happen to you there? I will tell you. As soon as you open your mouth and say you come from Nigeria everybody will hold fast to his purse. Is that a good thing?" The whole school shouted "No, sir!"

"That is what these nincompoops here have done to you." There was laughter again at *nincompoops,* another strange word.

Chike shivered to think that if he had had sixpence he would have stood there on the platform with the rest. He was sorry for Ezekiel and the others but especially for his good friend, S.M.O.G.

The headmaster was still speaking. He said that Samuel's punishment would be the lightest and Ezekiel's the heaviest. Samuel had merely begged for a camera; he had not made a false promise to send a leopard skin in return. But the headmaster reminded the school that begging was a bad thing by itself. He said, "A person who begs has no self-respect, he has no shame and no dignity. He is an inferior person. In this school we do not want to produce inferior people . . ."

Afterward Ezekiel was given twelve strokes of the cane and he cried. Samuel was given six strokes, and the others nine strokes each. Ezekiel's mother went to the headmaster's house that evening and rained abuses on him.

From that day on Ezekiel got new names in the school. Some called him Leopard Skin; others called him Scallywag or Scally-beggar. Only his closest friends still called him Tough Boy.

5

Those Who Answered to "Abraham"

After the incident of the leopard skin Chike lost some of his eagerness for crossing the Niger. He did not see how he could obtain one shilling without stealing or begging. His only hope now was that some kind benefactor might give him a present of one shilling without his begging for it. But where was such a man? he wondered. Perhaps the best thing was to take his mind off the River Niger altogether; but it was not easy.

On the last day of term all the pupils were tidying up the school premises. The boys cut the grass in the playing fields and the girls washed the classrooms. Chike's class was working near the mango tree with all the tempting ripe fruit which they were

forbidden to pick. They sang an old prisoners' work song and swung their blades to its beat. The last day of term was always a happy, carefree day; but it was also a day of anxiety because the results of the term's examination would be announced. Of course it was not a promotion examination. Still an examination was an examination and nobody liked to fail.

Chike heard the headmaster shout, "Abraham!" and stood up to see what was happening. Some other boys had also stood up. It was a trap. The headmaster picked out all those who had stood up and sent them to carry a missionary's luggage to the village of Okikpe.

"It is the price you have to pay for being overcurious," said the headmaster and he told them the proverb about the overcurious monkey who got a bullet in the brain.

Everyone laughed at the boys who had fallen into the headmaster's trap.

Okikpe was six miles away by road. Somewhere on this road there was a bridge across the River Nkisa. But this bridge had been washed away by heavy rains. The missionary's luggage was loaded into a lorry. The seven boys who had been picked out were to travel in the lorry as far as the bridge. Then they would get down and carry the loads across the stream and on to Okikpe, which was two miles from the river.

The boys were scared. But the driver of the lorry told them that the river was shallow at that point. Still they were afraid, especially Chike who did not know how to swim.

The lorry started and Chike felt like a condemned prisoner. Some of the older boys frightened him more by telling stories of people who had been drowned while fording the river.

"There are stones on the riverbed and if you miss your step once you are finished," said Mark.

Mark was a very big boy who was no good at his classwork. The other boys made fun of him and called him Papa.

"I know someone who went across it yesterday and he said it was five feet deep," continued Mark.

"I shall refuse to go across," said Chike.

"Well, you can wait with your own share of the luggage until they rebuild the bridge," said Mark, who was enjoying himself enormously. Some of the bigger boys laughed.

At last they got to the river and the lorry stopped.

Chike had taken a private decision to turn round if the water rose higher than his waist. After the luggage had been unloaded Mark said that it should be divided into seven equal loads. "After all we are all in the same class. We are all equal."

But the driver of the lorry was very kind and gave only a small basket to Chike.

Then each boy took off his clothes, wrapped them into a bundle, and carried them with the load on the head. Mark walked straight into the river and began to ford it. Some local people were coming over from the other side. A sudden feeling of defiance came upon Chike and he followed Mark. Some of the bigger boys who had been laughing and boasting were now hanging back. The water rose to Chike's chest at its deepest point but he did not turn back. Once he stepped on a slippery stone and nearly fell. But he quickly regained his balance. The water which had been growing deeper and deeper was now becoming shallow again. Chike was pleased with himself. Soon he was on dry ground. He turned round proudly to see the others struggling through.

The rest of the journey was uneventful. But the experience had been very important to Chike. It had given him a good deal of confidence in himself. He felt that any person who could ford a river deserved praise. There was one proverb which Chike's uncle was fond of saying: *It is bad that a man who has swum in the great River Niger should be drowned in its small tributary.* It means that a man who has passed a big test should not fail a small one. Chike made a new proverb of his own. He said: *A man who can walk through the Nkisa with his bare feet should not be afraid to sail the Niger in a boat.*

6
Brain Pills

Chike and the others got back to the school at about six in the evening. Of course the school had long closed. So they went to the headmaster's house to hear their results. Chike and two other boys passed but Mark and the other three failed. As soon as he heard his result Chike ran away as fast as he could for fear of being beaten by the disappointed and angry Mark.

As soon as he had run away to safety Chike slowed down to a walk. He remembered a poem their teacher had written:

> *There was a dull boy in our class*
> *Who swore: "At all costs I must pass."*

He read himself blind,
He cluttered up his mind
With pills; and was bottom of the class.

Teacher wrote this little poem when three foolish pupils nearly died from swallowing brain pills. Some dishonest trader had told the three boys that pills would help them to remember what they read. So they bought the harmful drugs from him and began to take them. But just before the examinations they were behaving like mad people and had to be rushed to the hospital.

They spent five days in hospital and were then discharged. The doctor said they were very lucky; they might have damaged their brains permanently. As for the examination the foolish boys had been so shaken that they failed hopelessly.

Chike recalled all the wild rumors that spread through the school at the time. Before the boys were discharged from hospital it was rumored that the doctor had pronounced them permanently insane. Another rumor said that one of the boys had slapped the headmaster when he had gone to see them. The source of this last rumor was Ezekiel.

Chike remembered how worn out the boys had looked the first day they returned to school. Everyone watched them closely for the least sign of unusual behavior. It was only after several days of watching that they were accepted as fully normal. By that time the examinations were already over and the holidays were near.

It must have been during the holidays that their teacher wrote the little poem which he made public at the beginning of the next term. By then several weeks had passed, and it was possible for everyone to laugh about the incident. Even the three unfortunate boys joined in.

Chike was now approaching home. He had turned off the tarred road and was walking on the sandy footpath which formed a shortcut to no. 15 Odu Street where he lived. He found a hard, unripe orange by the wayside and began to kick it along the path. He imagined himself as center-forward in a big match. He would dribble past an imaginary opponent and shout *Eh!* as spectators do when their favorite player outwits an opponent. Then he dribbled past three more and counted "One, two, three" before scoring an imaginary goal. "It's a goal!" he shouted, and threw his arms in the air.

Then he saw a shiny object which he had kicked up with a lot of sand. He bent down and picked it up. For a brief moment the world seemed to spin round him. He closed his eyes and then opened them again. Yes, it was there in his palm—a sixpence. He looked around to see if the owner of the money was coming behind. There was no one. He looked ahead; no one was in sight. He closed his hand on the coin and put the hand into his pocket. Then he walked boldly away. But soon he found himself running.

7

The Fate of the Coin

Chike had never had as much money as this before. The largest sum of money he had ever had at one time was threepence. That was at Easter when he had joined a group of other boys to make music.

The leader of the group was a masked dancer. In the custom of the people this masked dancer was regarded as a spirit. The other boys were called his disciples or attendants. Chike was one of the disciples.

Their instruments were very simple. They had one small but real drum made of wood and animal skin. The other drum was a biscuit tin beaten with a stick. Then a few rattles were made by shaking ciga-rette tins containing pebbles. Those who had no

instruments clapped their hands. The group went from house to house and sang for the inmates. Usually they were given a little money but sometimes they received food or biscuits. At the end of the day they had shared their earnings and Chike received threepence which he spent on groundnuts.

All this happened some time ago. Now Chike had become a different person. He had no desire to spend his money on groundnuts. He wanted to spend it in fulfilling his ambition. Of course sixpence was not enough; he needed one shilling for the trip. But as their teacher said, little drops of water make the mighty ocean. Thinking about this saying Chike remembered his mother's friend, Sarah, who sold snuff at Umuofia. Sarah was a great talker and her language was full of vivid pictures. She once told a story about a little bird and the River Niger. Chike so liked the story that he added bits to improve it. This is Chike's version of the story: Once there was a quarrel between a little bird and the River. The River was full of scorn and contempt for the size of the bird, and said: "Even the biggest bird in the air is beneath my notice. As for you, I think of you as a grain of sand. How long are you? Two inches. Do you know how long I am? Two thousand and six hundred miles! I come all the way from the Futa Jalon Mountains through five countries. Get out of my sight."

The little bird swooped down on the River and sipped a mouthful of water and swallowed it. Then he said to the River: "However great you may be I have now reduced you by a drop. You are smaller than you were this morning. Come and catch me if you can." And with that he flew away proudly. The River thought about it and decided that the little bird was right. And he realized too that there was one thing a river could not do. It could not fly.

Chike's interest in the River Niger probably began from the day he heard that story. Of course Sarah had told it much more simply. Chike had added the part about the length of the river, the five countries, and the name of the mountains. Geography was one of his favorite subjects and he liked to study his atlas.

Now to go back to the sixpence. Chike wrapped it carefully in a small piece of paper and put it in his school box. But after one week he began to think of ways of making the sixpence grow into a shilling. One way was to start trading with it. But what kind of trading could he do with such a small sum of money? In any case he knew that his uncle would not allow him to trade. In the end Chike took his problem to his friend Samuel, alias S.M.O.G. Samuel knew how to act like a grown-up. He sat down and began to think, his chin in his left hand.

"You want to change your sixpence into a shilling?" he asked.

"Yes," replied Chike.

"You can go to a money-doubler."

"Where does he live?"

"I don't know but I can find out for you, tomorrow."

So they agreed to go in search of a money-doubler on the following day. Meanwhile they decided to go and play. On their way they passed by people selling cooked guinea-fowl eggs and specially prepared meat called *suya*. An idea occurred to S.M.O.G. He had threepence in his pocket.

"Let us buy eggs and *suya*," he said. "If I buy threepence worth of *suya* and you buy threepence worth of eggs then I can have some of your eggs and you can have some of my *suya*."

"But the only money I have is for doubling," said Chike.

"You talk like a small boy," said S.M.O.G. "You will have threepence left which you can double to become sixpence and then double the sixpence to become one shilling."

"That is true," said Chike. "I can even double the shilling."

"Of course," said S.M.O.G.

"But why spend as much as threepence?" asked Chike. "Let us start with one penny each."

"Small-boy talk again," sneered S.M.O.G. "One penny will only buy one egg; threepence will buy four. Why should we have half an egg each when we can have two? Did we eat eggs yesterday? Why should we live by the River Niger and then wash our hands with spittle?"

Chike gave in. The proverb was very convincing. Chike had heard it used before about Peter Nwaba, the miserly trader. Someone said Mr. Nwaba lived on the Niger and yet washed his hands with spittle; he was very rich and yet lived like a pauper.

Chike did not care to be likened to Mr. Nwaba. So he gave in. He bought four eggs and received threepence change. He gave S.M.O.G. two of the eggs and put two in his pocket. Then they went in search of *suya*.

Chike felt like a grown man. He had never spent threepence at one blow and had never eaten a whole skewer of *suya* before. He had only eaten one or two small pieces given him by Ezekiel or S.M.O.G. Today he was going to eat a whole stick.

S.M.O.G. knew his way about and they soon found the *suya* people. Chike was fascinated by the way it was prepared. Small pieces of meat were skewered on a slender piece of stick. They were then dipped in a mixture of palm oil, pepper, groundnut, and salt. The sticks or spits were then stuck into the ground round an open fire which cooked the meat slowly.

S.M.O.G. paid threepence and took two hot and appetizing skewers. Chike almost danced with excitement. He wanted to start eating at once but S.M.O.G. insisted that they should go to the shade of a nearby mango tree.

"We must not eat like people without home-training, eating and walking along the street," he said.

Chike felt somewhat ashamed of himself and agreed with S.M.O.G. They sat on the exposed roots of a mango tree and began to munch their *suya,* pulling off the small pieces of meat from the spit with their teeth.

8

Chike Falls Out
with S.M.O.G.

When they had eaten the *suya*, S.M.O.G. suggested that they play a little game with their eggs. He knocked each of his eggs against his front teeth and from the sound decided which had the harder shell. He held it in his closed palm allowing the pointed end to show between his thumb and first finger. Then he asked Chike to knock one of his eggs against it.

"If your egg cracks it will become mine but if mine cracks I will give it to you," he said.

Chike tried each egg on his teeth and selected one. He rubbed its pointed end on his palm and then blew on it with his breath.

"Go on. Don't waste my time," said S.M.O.G.

Chike knocked his egg against his friend's. There was a sound of cracking, but at first it was not clear which one had broken. Chike looked at his and it was whole; then he saw that he had smashed S.M.O.G.'s. He leapt up in joy. Very sadly S.M.O.G. gave him the broken egg. Now he had only one. "Let us try the other two," suggested Chike. But S.M.O.G. refused.

"Get out!" he said angrily in English.

"Come in!" replied Chike, as he carefully removed the shell of the broken egg. "Why are you crying? You suggested the game."

"Who is crying?" said S.M.O.G. "Mind yourself," he added, again in English.

Chike laughed as he ate the egg he had won. S.M.O.G. broke his remaining egg against a mango root and began to eat it silently. Chike began to whistle a song about a boy who cries at play whenever the game goes against him.

S.M.O.G. stood up and began to look for something. Soon he picked up an overripe mango that lay on the ground. Something had eaten part of it and left a small round hole. S.M.O.G. held the fruit close to his ear, smiling. Then he gave it to Chike.

"There is something singing inside here. Listen to it."

Chike was suspicious and held the mango at arm's length.

"He is afraid," sneered S.M.O.G. "Does a mango bite? If it were eating eggs you would become bold."

Chike brought the fruit nearer to his ear. In doing so he closed the round hole with his palm. Then something stung him in the palm and he dropped the fruit and cried out at the same time.

S.M.O.G. laughed and laughed and laughed. "Bush boy," he said.

Chike's palm was smarting very badly and he kept rubbing and scratching it. Then he turned and began to go home, still scratching his palm. S.M.O.G. had a sudden change of mind. He went to Chike and said he was sorry. At first Chike ignored him. But S.M.O.G. persisted and very soon they were friends again. The pain from the bee's sting was much reduced. Before they got home Chike presented one of his eggs to S.M.O.G.

9

The Money-Doubler

The next day S.M.O.G. had to go to the General Hospital to see his sick mother. So he could not accompany Chike to the money-doubler. But he described carefully the way to the man's place and Chike set out on his own.

The place was not difficult to find. The signboard outside read:

PROFFESSOR CHANDUS

FAMOUS MARGICIAN, AND HERBALISTS

A TRIAL WILL CONVINSE YOU

He was a short man and wore a white singlet that had turned brown. His shorts were oversized. They were made from very hard material like tarpaulin and creaked when he sat down.

"What do you want?" he asked.

"I want you to double my money," said Chike.

"How much?" asked the man.

"Threepence."

"Three what?"

"Threepence," said Chike. "That is all I have."

"Ha ha ha ha ha. He has brought threepence to Professor Chandus. Ha ha ha ha ha!"

"That is all I have," said Chike again.

"All right," said Chandus. "I like you very much. What is your name?"

"Chike."

"Chike. I like you. What is your father's occupation?"

"My father is dead," replied Chike.

"Yes, I knew that but I wanted to test you," said Chandus.

Chike wondered how he knew. It showed he was a real magician.

"Professor Chandus does not double threepence but he will help you," he said. "I will give you something which will bring you plenty of money. Look at me."

Chike looked steadily at him. He brought out a

six-inch nail from one of his pockets and pushed it into his nostril until the whole length had disappeared.

"Call me Professor Chandus," he said.

"Professor Chandus," said Chike.

"That is my name. I am alpha and omega. Abracadabra. Pick up that piece of paper."

Chike picked up a small, dirty piece of paper from the floor and gave it to the man.

"Watch carefully," said Chandus. He squashed the paper between his palms and whispered something into the closed fist. Then he opened his hands and there was a small ring of wire there. He gave this to Chike.

"When you get home," said Chandus, "dip it in water seven times. Then put it under your pillow when you sleep. In the morning it will bring you plenty of money."

Chike took the ring and thanked Chandus and was about to go.

"The spirits want something from you," said Chandus.

"I have nothing but this threepence," replied Chike.

"It will do," said Chandus. "Tomorrow the spirits will reward you."

Chike reluctantly gave him the threepence.

When he got home he did as Chandus had told him. He dipped the ring in water seven times and placed it under his pillow when he went to sleep. He woke up twice in the night thinking it was dawn. On the second occasion he woke up Michael and asked if it was morning yet. Michael grumbled angrily and warned Chike not to disturb his sleep again.

When morning finally came Chike was sleeping peacefully and deeply and Michael had to shake him vigorously to wake him up.

He sat up, grumbling and rubbing his eyes. There was something on his mind but he could not say what it was. Then, like a flash, his mind went to the ring. He pushed aside his pillow. The ring lay on the mat as nakedly as he had left it.

10

Chike Returns to Chandus

Throughout that morning Chike was very unhappy. He barely touched his breakfast. Michael asked him what was wrong but he said nothing and went on brooding.

By midday he decided to go and report the matter to S.M.O.G. After all it was he that recommended the magician to Chike.

S.M.O.G. was eating garri and okro soup. The front of his shirt was covered with the soup, which he found difficult to control. Chike noticed the quantity of fish in the soup and his throat began to itch.

"Come and join me," said S.M.O.G. with his mouth full.

"No, thank you," said Chike. "I am not hungry."

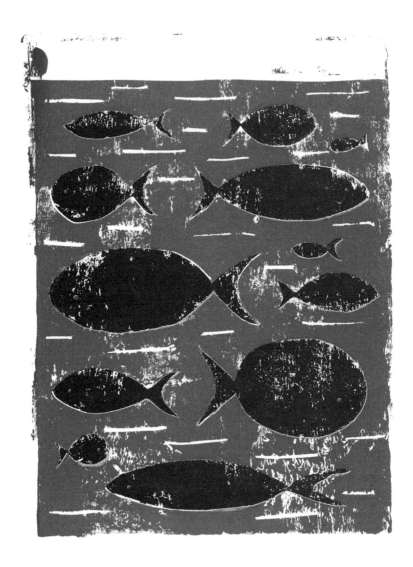

"Go and join him," said S.M.O.G.'s father who was reclining on a stretcher.*

Chike did not need any more persuading. He washed his hands and fell to. He knew how to control okro soup and when he had finished eating, his shirt was hardly soiled.

Chike did not want S.M.O.G.'s father to hear about the magician; so he took S.M.O.G. outside before telling him what had happened.

S.M.O.G. appeared very unhappy about it all. He swore he was going to teach the fellow a lesson.

"Has he ever doubled money for you?" asked Chike.

"No," replied S.M.O.G. "I get everything I need from my mother. So I don't need to have my money doubled."

Chike was not impressed by this argument but did not wish to pursue it.

"How is your mother?" he asked.

"She is getting better," said S.M.O.G. "It is her rheumatism."

"What is rheumatism?" asked Chike.

"I don't know. It is something old people get. Her legs are painful."

The two set out for the magician's house. Chike

* Hammock.

said they must hurry because he wanted to be back before his uncle returned from work.

"Did you tell him?" asked S.M.O.G.

"No," said Chike. "How can I tell him?"

When they got to Chandus's place he was eating coconut with garri soaked in water.

"What do you want?" he asked with great annoyance.

"I am Chike who came yesterday."

"Me I no understand you," said Chandus in pidgin.

"But you gave me this ring," said Chike, producing the wire ring.

"Me give you dat? You de craze?"

"I sent him to you," said S.M.O.G., "and he gave you his threepence to double for him."

"Wonders will never end," said Chandus. "You two come here and give me threepence."

"I did not come with him but . . ."

"Make una come ot from here one time or I go learn you lesson you no fit forget. Imagine! Why small boys of nowadays no de fear. You get bold face to come my house and begin talk rubbish. Na your father steal threepence no be me. Stand there when I come back and you go see." He rushed into an inner room and scraped a machete on the hard floor. S.M.O.G. took to his heels and Chike followed.

11

Pride Goeth Before a Fall

Chike's friend Samuel, alias S.M.O.G., began to teach him how to ride a bicycle during the holidays. Samuel had no bicycle himself but he could easily borrow one from a mechanic. This mechanic lived in one of the rooms in Samuel's father's house. During the day he worked under a tree in front of the house. Many people brought their bicycles to him to be repaired. Sometimes they wanted the brakes mended or a punctured tire repaired. Whatever it was the mechanic was equal to the job. If you passed by at any time of the day, you would see him in his brown, greased work clothes putting life into a damaged bicycle. Usually he turned the bicycle upside down with its wheels in the air while he worked on it. He had a signboard nailed to the tree on which was written his nickname—DOCTOR OF BICYCLES.

Besides the bicycles which came to him for repairs the mechanic also had about five or six of his own which he let out on hire for sixpence an hour. It was one of these that Samuel borrowed. He did not tell the mechanic that a learner was going to ride it. If the mechanic had been told, he would surely have refused.

The bicycle was for adults and was too high for Chike but he made rapid progress. If he sat on the seat his feet would not reach the pedals. So he adopted what was called the monkey-style; he rode standing on the pedals on one side of the triangular frame.

After about one week of practice Chike was able to ride long distances without falling down. He was even able to whistle a song as he rode along. Samuel was impressed with Chike's progress and suggested that it was time he tried riding on the main road instead of the playing field. As Samuel said, the real test of a good cyclist was the main road.

Chike was a little doubtful at first but he agreed in the end to try one of the less busy roads. To his surprise he did very well. He was so pleased that he began to whistle the highlife tune "Nike Nike" and to pedal to its beat. He felt very proud of himself and wondered why people said that riding a bicycle was difficult. *It is easier than eating okro soup,* thought Chike. Just then a car came out of a side street and was making toward Chike. He lost his nerve and swerved into the curb, hitting an electric pole. The bicycle bounced back and threw Chike into a nearby drain. He came out dripping with dirty water. He had also grazed his elbow and knee on the cement curb. But the wound was not deep.

The bicycle, however, seemed to be badly damaged. The front wheel was twisted and its brakes were jammed. Three spokes were also broken. Chike and Samuel tried in vain to straighten up the wheel. In the end they gave up and decided to go and report to the mechanic. Since the front wheel refused to revolve they lifted it off the ground and rolled the bicycle home on the back wheel.

The mechanic was very angry. He said that Chike must pay for the damage.

"But I have no money," said Chike. "Please forgive him; he has no money," said Samuel. But the mechanic replied, "If he has no money, who asked him to ride my bicycle? Come and show me where you live. If you have no money your parents must pay for your foolishness."

Chike begged and pleaded but the mechanic would not hear. He said, "You are wasting my time. Come on and show me your father and mother. If you don't hurry up I shall take you to the police station right now."

So Chike led the way and the mechanic followed, riding slowly on one of his bicycles. Chike was afraid of taking the man to his uncle. So he decided to take him round and round the town. They went up one street, down the next, and up the third.

"Where do you say you live?" asked the mechanic.

"I don't know the number," said Chike. "But it is over there," and he pointed in front of him.

After a long time they were back where they started. The mechanic was now furious and was threatening to beat hell out of Chike. Because he was so furious he did not look where he was going and ran into a woman returning from the market with her purchases. Her enormous basket fell down on the road and the contents were scattered. She immediately took off her headcloth and tied it firmly round her waist, ready for a fight. She held the mechanic by his shirt and was shouting abuses into his face.

"I had twenty pounds' worth of goods in that basket. Give it to me now."

Crowds were gathering. Some people were picking up the woman's things and putting them back into the basket. There were tomatoes, some dried fish, and small yams. But her voice rose higher and higher. She said she was not going home to prepare a meal from things picked off the road. She wanted her twenty pounds.

In the confusion Chike melted away and ran home faster than he had ever done before.

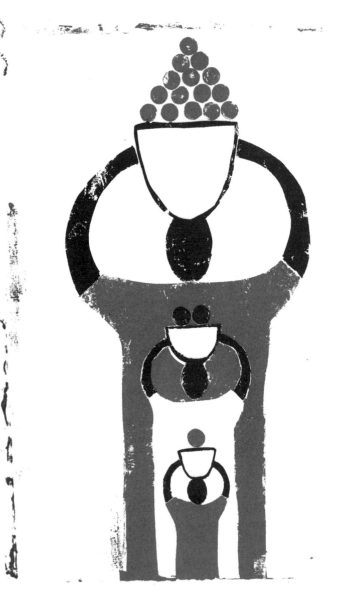

12

The Miserly Trader

Chike did not entirely give up hopes of crossing the River Niger. But it now seemed more unlikely than ever that he would find the money. So he thought, what was the use of dreaming? As his mother used to say: *A poor man should not dream of rice.*

One day Chike saw Mr. Nwaba counting bundles and bundles of pound notes. He had not known that so much money existed in the world. If Mr. Nwaba had so much, Chike thought, why did he live so miserably? He lived in one room with his wife and five children. They ate hardly anything else but garri. If his wife put much fish in the soup he would rave and curse. Sometimes he even beat her. His children wore threadbare clothes to school and were always  last to pay their school fees. He rode an old rickety bicycle for which he never bought a license. Whenever he heard that policemen were stopping cyclists to check their licenses, he put his old machine away for a week or two. His neighbors called him Money-Miss-Road behind his back.

Chike was so desperate for money that he began to hope that this miser might give it to him. So when Mr. Nwaba came home from his stalls in the evening of the next day Chike went out and said "Good evening, sir" to him and rolled in his bicycle.

Mr. Nwaba seemed very pleased. He returned Chike's greeting with "Good evening, my son" and a broad smile. For about a week Chike did the same thing every evening. But Mr. Nwaba never seemed to think of giving him anything except once when he dipped his hand into the pocket of his khaki trousers. Chike's heart beat with expectation. Mr. Nwaba brought out his hand again and gave Chike three groundnuts.

Mr. Nwaba was always thinking of profit and loss and doing sums in his mind. One day Chike greeted him with "Good morning, sir." He replied, "Five pounds."

His full name was Mr. Peter Nwaba. He was well known in the town and went to church regularly. Every Sunday morning he put on his gorgeous *agbada* and went with his family to the nearby church, and every Friday he went to the Bible class. Chike always wondered how such a cruel man could pay so much attention to religion.

Sometimes Mr. Nwaba left his room very late at night and would not come back till the following day. People said he belonged to a secret society which met only at night.

One night Chike had an upset stomach after eating unwashed mangoes. At about four o'clock in the morning he got up to go to the latrine. As he opened the door he heard footsteps outside. He held the door nearly closed and peeped out. It was Mr. Nwaba and another strange man returning from somewhere. They stood outside and talked for a while. Then the stranger went away and Mr. Nwaba retired to his room.

Chike did not give much thought to this incident at the time. But he was to remember it later.

13

Chike's Dream Comes True

Chike's chance came suddenly. It happened on a public holiday. His uncle had gone to Umuofia for the holiday and was not expected back until the next day. Chike ate his lunch quickly and went down to the riverside without saying a word to Michael. Since he had no money he did not think of crossing the river. All he wanted to do was to watch the boats.

When he got to the bank he found many cars and lorries waiting to be ferried. Then he saw three boys with buckets of water washing some of the cars. He saw also that when they had finished the owners gave them some money. Why did I not think of this before? he asked himself. He raced back home and took a bucket and a piece of rag and ran all the way back. To his utter disappointment the boat had gone and there were no more cars around, only lorries. But soon other cars began to arrive and Chike's hopes revived. So far three had arrived. But they were all very small cars. Chike thought it would be better to go for a big one with a wealthy owner. Soon an enormously long car pulled up. Chike immediately approached it.

The owner looked like a very important person. Perhaps he was a minister. Then Chike lost his boldness. He stood by the car wondering what to say. But while he hesitated one of the other boys marched up to the man and said, "May I wash your car, sir?"

At first the man ignored him but he did not give up. He spoke again, "Oga, your car dorty plenty. I fit wash am fine."

This time the man looked at him and nodded. The boy smiled and set to work. Chike bit his lips. He said to himself, *If this boy can do it so can I.*

Then one small car arrived. Chike, no longer choosy, wasted no time at all. He went up to the owner and said in good English, "May I wash your car, sir? It is very dirty and you are going to Lagos."

The man smiled and said, "Go ahead."

Chike filled his bucket with water from a nearby tap and set to work.

When he had finished he told the owner. But the man was busy talking to his friend and paid little attention to Chike. He said "Thank you" without looking at Chike and continued talking. Chike stood there, shifting from one foot to the other. Eventually the man looked at him again and put his hand into his pocket. Chike's heart beat faster. He brought out a handful of coins and gave one to Chike.

"Thank you, sir," said Chike. Then he looked at the coin and saw that it was one shilling. In his joy he said again, "Thank you, sir." The man did not reply; he was talking to his friend again, with a cigarette in his mouth.

14

Chike on the Boat

Chike's dream had come true; at last he could go to Asaba. He jumped up and down several times and sang "One More River to Cross." It was one of the songs he had learnt at the C.M.S. Central School, Umuofia.

He joined the queue of other passengers. When his turn came he gave the shilling to the cashier who gave him a ticket and sixpence change. His heart was aglow with happiness. After today he would be able to say to his friends, "I too have been to Asaba. There only remains Lagos."

The next ferry was a long time coming. Chike became very impatient. He walked up and down, whistling:

Leave your wife and join the Army
One more river to cross;
One more river, one more river,
One more river to cross.

At last the ferryboat was coming. It looked very small in the distance. Chike's heart beat like a hammer. He sat down on one of the long wooden seats, then stood up again. He turned away from the approaching boat in the hope that when he looked again it would be much nearer. He shut his eyes and counted up to two hundred. He did everything he could think of to make the time pass more quickly.

At long last the boat arrived. Passengers from Asaba began to stream out, some of them carrying head-loads. After the passengers, the cars and lorries came out one by one.

Many of the cars were covered with brown dust from their long journey. So there was dust on the Lagos road, thought Chike. He had not expected that. Such a great road should be free from dust, he thought.

When the vehicles from Asaba had all left the ferry the vehicles from Onitsha began to drive on. Sometimes it looked as if a car or lorry would fall into the river. But none did. Chike saw the car he had washed enter the boat. It looked very clean and new. He had already memorized its number, PC 7379.

The last car to go in had a radio blaring out at full volume. Its owner was not there and so the chauffeur was having fun. He was even offering to take passengers to Lagos at a moderate charge. When this last car had boarded the boat a marine official in a white-and-blue uniform waved the passengers on. Immediately there was a big rush for the deck. Chike was in the forefront of this rush.

The ferry's engine started. The siren sounded above. Then a bell rang in the engine room. It sounded like a giant bicycle bell. The boat began to move backward. When it was clear of the ground the bell rang again and the engine increased its sound. Then the boat swung round and began its journey to Asaba.

It was all like a dream. Chike wondered whether it was actually happening. *So this is me,* he thought. *Chike Anene, alias Chiks the Boy, of Umuofia, Mbaino District, Onitsha Province, Eastern Nigeria, Nigeria, West Africa, Africa, World,*

Universe. This was how he wrote his name in his new reader. It was one of the things he had learnt from his friend Samuel, alias S.M.O.G.

During the journey Chike felt as proud as Mungo Park when he finally reached the Niger. Here at last was the great River Niger. Chike stuck out his chest as though he owned the river, and drew a deep breath. The air smelt clean and fresh. He remembered another song he had learnt at Umuofia and began to whistle it:

> *Row, row, row your boat*
> *Gently down the stream*
> *Merrily, merrily, merrily, merrily,*
> *Life is but a dream.*

When he became tired of whistling he began to think of Lagos. He wondered what Carter Bridge looked like. He had heard it described on the radio. He also knew of Tinubu Square, the marina, Tafawa Balewa Square, Bar Beach, Yaba, Apapa, statehouse, and so on. But the place he wanted to see most of all was the City Stadium where all those football matches were played. Chike liked nothing more than a football commentary broadcast by the N.B.C. Whenever there was a match some of the neighbors would come to listen on his uncle's radio. They all admired the commentator. When he cried, "It's a goal!" everyone shouted, "It's a goal!" Some would even jump to their feet and shake hands with their friends. Of course they only did so when their favorite team scored.

15

Chike Is in Trouble

At last the ferryboat arrived in Asaba and the passengers rushed out. Chike looked around him. He could not believe his eyes. Was this Asaba about which he had heard so much? There was nothing to see except a few miserable-looking houses. He was really disappointed. He joined the other passengers and climbed the steep ascent to the market. Things brightened up there. But he had expected more. The market could not be compared to the one in Onitsha. There was nothing here like Bright Street where the noise of highlife records drowned the noise of cars. He walked beyond the market with his hands in his pockets, looking this way and that like a European inspector of schools.

From the stories his friends told Chike expected Asaba to be better than any place he had seen. And he expected the Midwestern region to be very different from the East. But now the air felt the same, the soil had the same look, and the people went about their business in the same manner. As Chike went farther inland he saw better houses. But still they were nothing to write home about; they were all inferior to the fine buildings on New Market Road at Onitsha.

Anyhow, Chike was happy about one thing. He could now talk like the rest of his companions.

Evening was setting in. Chike thought he had seen enough of Asaba and must now go back. He felt in his pocket for his sixpence and found it. He turned round and began to walk back to the riverside. The distance seemed to have increased. Chike began to run. But when he got to the bank the boat was gone. He could see it in the distance. It was already halfway to Onitsha. Chike was in a panic. He saw a marine official closing up his office. He ran to him and said with a shaking voice, "Please, sir, I want to return to Onitsha."

"You want to return to Onitsha?" asked the man,

searching his pocket for keys. He sounded helpful and kind. Chike's hopes returned.

"Yes, sir," he replied.

"I am sorry but you cannot return to Onitsha today," said the man. "The last boat has gone. Come back tomorrow morning."

"But I live in Onitsha," cried Chike. "I know nobody here."

"I am sorry," said the man as he locked the door of his office and walked away.

Chike stood there weeping. Then one man who had been bathing in the river came up with a towel around his waist and said, "To come Asaba no hard but to return." He looked very dangerous and wicked; Chike became really afraid and decided to go away from the riverside. With his head bowed and tears in his eyes he returned to the Asaba market. There he leaned against one of the old lorries and wept silently. He wished he had obeyed his mother and never gone near the river. Then he remembered another thing his mother always said. She told her children that crying does not solve any problem. So instead of crying Chike began to think and plan.

His first thought was to go to the owner of one of the shops and ask if he could sleep there. But then it occurred to him that the man might be a thief and kidnapper. Finally Chike decided to hide inside one of the old lorries until morning. He inspected them and saw that one was called *S.M.O.G. no. 1*. He decided to sleep in it because of its good and friendly name.

16
Chike's Troubles Grow

Chike did not want to go into the lorry while people were looking. So he decided to walk around until it was quite dark. He saw traders closing their shops and market women packing up their wares to return home. Soon the market was almost empty. Dusk was followed by darkness. Chike went to the back of the lorry and climbed in quietly. At first he lay down on one of the benches. Then he thought it was better to hide under them. So he climbed under the benches and lay on the floor of the lorry. He thought of his mother and sisters quite safe at home and his misery grew. He was hungry and mosquitoes sang in his ear. He did not try to kill them because they were too many and because killing them would make a noise. He coiled himself up with one hand as pillow and the other between his knees. He could not sleep because of fear. Several times he thought he heard footsteps approaching. He prayed and cried quietly in the darkness.

After a long time he fell asleep. But it was not a restful sleep. He was troubled by bad dreams. He dreamt of all kinds of evil men and spirits chasing him and screaming in his ears.

Then in the middle of the night he woke up suddenly. Three men were talking very close to him. His body froze with fear. The men were actually leaning on the lorry. Chike could hear their bodies rubbing against the wood. They spoke in low voices, sometimes in Ibo and sometimes in pidgin English. Chike could hear every word they said.

"He is expecting us when the church bell rings three o'clock," said one of them.

"Are you quite sure that he is trustworthy?" asked a second man.

"Yes," said the first man. "I trust him."

"You know that some of them can make arrangements with you and then go and tell the police," said the second man again. "We must be quite sure that he is trustworthy."

"Oga, if we no sure," said a third voice in pidgin, "make we no go at all. I no de for police wahala."

"You people too fear," said the first man. "Small thing you begin de shake like woman. Na only when time come for chop money person go know say you get power."

"Oga, no be say we de fear," said the second man, "but Oyibo people say prevention is better than cure."

"To get rich no easy; na for inside rock money build im house. If fight come we go fight. Dis revolver way I hol for hand no be for yeye?" said the man they called Oga.

Chike was now afraid even to breathe. He knew that if he made the slightest noise they would shoot him so he kept as quiet as a mouse.

As the men talked and made plans the church bell struck three. "Oya, make we go," said the first man, "by God power everything go all right."

Chike was happy when he heard "make we go." But his happiness vanished when he heard someone climbing into the back of the lorry. He opened his mouth to scream but no sound came out. Sweat covered his body and his throat was dry. He shut his eyes tight and waited for the worst.

The engine of the lorry started and it began to move. Chike opened his eyes a little but it was too dark to see. He closed them again. His body was now trembling.

The strange man at the back of the lorry with him began to cough and mutter something to himself. Because of his terror Chike did not know how long they had been traveling. But he knew when the lorry slowed down. Then it took a turning and went very slowly for a while before it stopped finally.

17

What the Thieves Did

When the lorry stopped the man at the back climbed out. Chike opened his eyes but it was pitch dark. The three men were now talking in whispers. Then the driver reversed the lorry.

For a while there was silence. Chike prayed that the men would move away for even one minute so that he could get down and hide. But they did not move. Instead a fourth man came and joined them. From what they said Chike understood that this fourth person was the night-watchman.

The first man, who seemed to be the leader of the thieves, spoke to the night-watchman.

"You see this gun way I carry," he said, "I no carry

am for play. If you start any turn-turn game na we and you go die."

"Why I go play you turn-turn game?" asked the watchman. "You tink money de bitter for my mout? Or you tink na dis watch-night work I go take send my pickin for college?"

"Oya, come show us the door," said the leader. Then he told the driver, whose name was Ignatius, to move out the benches from the back of the lorry. Chike was half-dead. He heard the man let down the tail-gate. But he did not come in. Instead he returned to the front of the lorry to get a flashlight. In the twinkling of an eye Chike slipped out and began to walk away. He had no idea where he was going. It was too dark to see. But he continued walking as quietly as a cat. Unfortunately his foot kicked against a tin and made a noise.

The driver shouted, "Who dat?"

Chike turned sharply to his left and ran. His eyes were now used to the darkness and he could see vaguely. He saw something like a door and walked in.

"I say who dat?" shouted the driver again and shined a flashlight.

There was very little room where Chike had entered. He felt about with his hands and found that the thing was like a big box with an open door.

He wanted to get out again and run. But the other men had joined the driver. He was telling them that while he was looking for his flashlight he heard a man's footsteps.

Chike shut his eyes and bit his lips. The men were looking for him. The night-watchman told them that no man would be walking around there at that hour. He said perhaps it was the cat which lived in one of the old houses. This reassured them and they all went away again. Chike's heart continued to pound like a pestle in a mortar.

Later he heard the men loading things into the lorry. It took them a very long time. But in the end the engine started and the lorry moved away. Chike heaved a great sigh of relief. He felt like singing. Then he remembered the night-watchman; he must be somewhere quite near. Chike's happiness vanished again. He prayed to God to send daylight and save him. As if in answer to his prayer a cock crowed somewhere in the distance. Another answered from the opposite direction.

But Chike did not know when dawn came. He was so tired that he had fallen asleep, standing.

18

How It All Ended

For the second time Chike was awakened by the voices of people. He opened his eyes in terror. To his great joy it was daylight. He came out of the huge box and peeped in the direction of the voices. They were loud and friendly. So he went toward the crowd. He was amazed by what he saw. A man was tied to a mango tree. His hands were tied behind him and his mouth was covered with a black cloth. He could neither move nor speak.

The crowd was very excited. Someone tried to untie the man but the others said it was best to wait for the police. Chike was thinking very hard. But he could not understand what was happening. His mind was confused and tired.

At last two policemen arrived and the man was untied. He fell down to the ground and Chike thought he was dead. Someone brought cold water and they poured it on him. This seemed to help because he raised himself and sat down.

It took him a long time to recover fully and to tell his story. All the time Chike was thinking as hard as he could. Everybody waited to hear the story of the man who had just been untied.

When he had rested he drank some water. Then he told his story. He said he was watching the big shop when a band of armed robbers attacked him and overpowered him. They tied him to the tree and then broke into the shop. He said they were about eight in number and that they came in a new lorry.

The policemen were about to go and look at the shop when a small boy suddenly shouted from the crowd.

"The man is telling lies," cried the boy. "I saw them."

All eyes were turned on the small boy. It was Chike.

"What is he talking about?" asked some people.

"I saw the thieves," said Chike. "This man helped them. I heard him talking with them."

Perhaps some people would have ignored Chike if

the watchman had not then behaved violently. As soon as he heard what Chike said he rushed forward and seized him by the throat. But one of the policemen saved Chike and pushed the man aside. The crowd was now angry with him for his violence.

"Do you want to kill the boy?" asked some of them. "It seems the boy has spoken the truth," said the others.

The policemen asked Chike what he meant. He was so excited that he could not tell the story well. But he told enough to convince everyone that he spoke the truth. He told them that the lorry was called *S.M.O.G. no. 1* and that its driver was called Ignatius. Then he showed them where he had hidden after his escape from the lorry. It was a sentry-box in a nearby garage.

As Chike told his story the night-watchman began to shake. He covered his face with his hands to hide his tears.

Chike became a hero. One big man in the crowd lifted him up and placed him on his shoulders. The others applauded. They said they had never seen such bravery from such a little boy.

The police arrested the three thieves that same day. They also recovered the bales of velvet they had stolen. The cloth was worth thousands of pounds. The manager of the shop shook hands with Chike and promised to make him a present later. Then he gave him a good meal and drove him in his car to the ferry.

Everywhere people spoke of Chike's adventure. His photograph appeared in the local newspaper and his name was mentioned on the radio. Then, after the three thieves and the night-watchman had been tried and imprisoned, Chike got a letter from the manager of the shop. He announced that the company which owned the shop had decided to award a scholarship to Chike which would take him right through secondary school.

So Chike's adventure on the River Niger brought him close to danger and then rewarded him with good fortune. It also exposed Mr. Peter Nwaba, the rich but miserly trader. For it was he who had led the other thieves.